THE SEVENTH TASK

SUKHVIR SONI

This book is dedicated to popular survival story and some science and psychological series.

If you don't really want to read the book now you can count the dots in the next pages till the introduction page and write how many were you able to find at the page before intro...

....

....

....

....

....

....

....

....

Contents

Foreword

....

....

....

....

....

....

Preface

....

....

....

....

....

....

....

....

Acknowledgements

....

....

....

....

....

....

....

....

Prologue

....

....

....

....

....

....

....

TOTAL DOTs =

Introduction

It's time my eyes opens to be closed again, we find ourselves trapped in a place that doesn't seem to stop changing. In order to survive you must pass the 7 tasks, it's going to be something you can't expect if you try. For experiment they made us suffer with many more, it made us ready for the danger at the center of the core. We have our smart brains and different skills joint together to coordinate cause that's the only way. Glasses shatter, the sun rise! games we play for the faith that ahead lies. Get excited you guys, for a journey you could never have imagined in a 100 billion years!!!

1

An Ordinary Day

Time passes slow as the Dart flows with the air, moving straight towards it's Target, and I see it. It hit it after spending an hour probably I got it, a bullseye! Hi let me introduce myself, I am Jack and I am not a pirate! An intresting person I happens to be, fairly powerful with almost unlimited power, just don't see the muscles. I have a vacation ahead, they don't teach much in school, what can you expect it's 169bc we still have a lot to evolve! Just joking it's 2022 and lockdown just ended here! I just really want to go back to the somewhere near 150bc and see what happened there with my big eyes. Oh little introduction, I am 12years in age, people say I have grown up but it still seems to me that I have been left behind. Like I just want to enjoy a bit, a bit more, I have a lazy schedule but it's better than many others. Cause you know I don't play video games 5 to 6 hours a day instead I just play 3 to 4. I know, me too want to do something new and intresting. It was time when I realized 3hours, 3hours has passed when I was trying to score a bullseye. Hey hey, before you think who takes this much time to score a bullseye, I want to say I took washroom, food even water breaks so deducte some time.

It was past 11AM and yeah I woke up early today. Walking down I was on my way to nowhere, I mean I had no idea where I was going, just outside taking the rays of the warm sun. I was walking while playing with a ball I found in home and wondering that could it work. Like I thought it was 1hour but it was 3, while I was trying to score a bullseye. So an hour of mine is equal to three hours in real time, that means for me studying one hour in school would be equal to three hours of studies for everyone else. Only if it works I would spend 3hours everyday studying and do it for a week and "whala" I get a three months vacation.

I was walking and talking alone with my useless mathematics when something scared me. Nah no monster it was just a friend, tell me if he's less. "Hi why you doin!" he asked. No words, is that the first question you ask when you meet somebody I said in my mind. Aye, it's the first day of we'res vacation what you do plan! he asked. What vacation, I thought your vacation is going on ever since, I mean you don't study right, especially grammer I replied. Did I made him disappointed? Well it's kind of on his face! Ok lets restart it all over from the beginning again he said with weird facial expressions. Where is spike! I was surely surprised with his grammer but the thing that surprised me more was what he said. Spike! my pet I cried. Where is he, you'll are always with each other he said. I know, Byeee! I will be sure to lend you a grammer book in future I said and left, leaving him confused and maybe furious. There I reached home, didn't took that long, my home was just a 50m away from where I was before. But then the thing I saw scared me, it was about my pet! A snake almost 2m in height with needle like spikes all around, sharp venomous teeth and not so scary look I would say, was right in front of it.

Ok wait that sharp tooth, spiky body and dangerous venomous snake is my pet and it was sitting in front of a mirror. You see, him in front of a mirror can be catastrophic some times. I grabbed him and ran out again, "Hiisss" he did and I replied, sorry to forget about you, realized it fast, didn't I. Then something scared me again. It was him again, I asked were you waiting for me? and he replied No Jake, I wanted to see spike. This sentence made me screamed on him, "My name is Jake not Jack", "No the opposite!" Spike "hissed" and he was gone. He ran away, you have got some power I told him. (Hiya guys! if you are interested to know about spike, my snake pet, this is the place. First things first he is a reptile! Atheris hispida is specific, he is venomous and by he you understand it's a boy. He is young 3years old and have a strong bond with Jack) So now what to our boy asked annddd a minute pause. Come on there could be something I can do, something I wanted to do. That was when he hissed, he got it and replied to his pet, "Good idea". I will work on going back to 150bc, In my own way. I mean I bought books, so reading books about barbarians with cool bg music is what to do. But little later, there is an apple tree nearby and we both love apple, not when mom gives us. There I had a munch, after spike and we were good. There was nobody outside, a clear way to home, little weird. I was just going upstairs when something scared me! It was mom, she said "Grab an apple from the basket."

Pitty me, I would be full for lunch, now I regret eating that big cheese balls while darting. But orders are order, so no choice. Having spikes' back, mostly in eating I was up and ready, ahh Almost. Then in robotic speed, AC on, windows close and bags of chocolates and chips(even though I am full). Now I was truely ready! Hopping inside the blanket with headphones on and book in front. I started reading with some lofi beats in bg. It is just about time, no food touched, no moment and most importantly no concentration for 3 minutes and here I am asleep. Like pet like owner! I really wanted to learn more about barbarians and stuff around tht time. It took more than usual for me to wake up this time and nobody waked me up. And when I say long I mean it, I was up at 2, 2 in the morning. That's a lot of time I said, and alone went for a walk with some chips and a coke I wasn't supposed to drink. Silent street! I said. Well to be honest I have no idea why I was out this night alone. I truely wanted to go back but just was not able to somehow. So I kept walking, I was far away now and I was holding the empty can. Just when I finished eating, I heard it, A sound grumpy and loud, if you havn't guessed it yet, it was ny stomach. With a weird face I said like how, I just finished eating. Leaves were moving, it was dark everywhere and I could feel something, it was hallucinations. These were frecking me out and I had no idea what to do, so. I stopped at a nearby house and made sure it was no creepy and located away from others. I rang the bell and waited in horror, then it opened. There were to figure one small and other little bigger and more creepy. The old lady came ahead in the moonlight and that was it.

"Ahhhhhhhhhhhhhhhhhhhhh", I screamed and ran as fast as I could. I was sure I was in the place of dead, I thought and ran for my life. Umm, It was actually a girl whoes name I keep forgetting's grandmother and what more she was wearing some kind of mask and a devilish cap thing. I bet I would have brock some records cause I never ran so fast. It was home were I stopped and yeah, I was running with eyes close in order to not see some creepy-horror real life thing and have nightmare's. My screech got lower when I was home and here back to bed with lights open and good songs playing, that's what I do in these situations. I had no idea what was that demonic thing, well not till now. Then again something unbelievable happend, I was deep in sleeep under 2 minutes, I at least knew one thing, "something was wrong."

It was 7 in the morning and something scared me, It was mom with a flash in the dark room. The first thing I saw after waking up was her face reflecting the light of the flash. I screamed "Lizard Lady, Lizard Lady", it annoyed her and here I get pushed back only to finally realize it was her. Get ready, I am waiting for the breakfast down. This morning I had a different energy and I went to shower. In the middle I remembered the past night incident which led me to the crazy and dark dream I had. Thinking about it made me weak and I sat down restlessly. It was like the time stopped and I could not remember or think anything anymore. I came out looking down and bumped into mom. She said it has been more than an hor it is way more than usual, sre you alright. Do you forgot you have to go meet everybody from school. And that hit me I forgot about everything ate some, ok alot of food and rushed to meet my friends with spike. I was there in time half an hour late is fine! There he called my back "45 minutes late huh", ok but I am here! It was Ben one of my 5 best friend. I turned back and was glad to see them all, spike was too. Yeah how are you guys? I asked. We sure are no sleepyheads said Harlow.

He all then sat on the small grass and had a little talk. We are a group of 6 friends, Benjamin, Harlow, Annabelle, Logan, Skylar and me! We all are of almost same year and i am the youngest amongst all have a difference of 9 months from the second youngest one! 3 of them are already teenagers!!!

I then told them what happened and they were up with their own theories. I told all that I have to find that girl and ask what was that. We were talking when a girl knocked my back, it was her the girl from the haunted house. She asked me what was I doing outside her house at night. This proof that the lady was not a monster and instead her grandmother, now was I relieved. Nothing I told and when I was finding an excuse she burst out a laugh. She told you were so scared seeing her and you ran screaming and continued laughing. Seeing her laugh my friends gave out a laugh too and I knew I am going to get stopped again and again today. Looking them all laugh everybody joined them and laughed out loud, embarrassing I know. It all stopped and she was leaving by waving bye when I asked what is your name again. Calista she replied and with a smile she left, now you know why I keep forgetting her name.

This was a meeting prepared by all the student when in school. I was meeting everybody I find which took sometimes then we had a big treat. My stomach was full and we 6 were walking around the streets of our city, seeing the fresh view around. Logan said, we have our vacation so what should we do now? Skylar replied Nobody is going out for this week at least so we have our time. Annabelle asked till when everybody has to go back home? In which I replied anytime and everybody agreed even when they know it was not quite true. We six were walking and talking from half an hour now, and it was when it started to happen. The weather changed and no one could we see around, it was like we were alone, we six. It is that house again I let them know with some fear. So this is the place you ran away, it's pretty far from your house Ben said. Skylar added Yeah what were you doing here 2AM in the dark, No I was talking about how could you keep a coke can filled for so long

Ben said. The weather was darkish blue and the sun was covered behind and no where to be seen. And then we could see something, a person covered in dark cloak. It looked like a women or a evil witch with her wooden stick. It was coming for them, Annabelle spoke up. You guys remember it is an old legend which represent witchcraft and rituals. It also says some tragic events like a city covered in water, a tornado, hot fire all around, a volcanic eruption and droughts, Earth blasting like swallowing people. The people with their dark magic torturing people with no powers and testing their intelligence. I stopped her and let them know that I almost passed out in between, good thing spike is with us. She was a feet away from us when she gave a bloody glare and surpassed us like nothing. We all looked behind and that thing scared me, she was waiting for us turn and we just did.

Then we hear a spooky voice from under the cloak really her voice is like a nightmare I said in mind. She said Six sweet we have, lets check what you all have got. Spike in full speed went to bite her but I was there to pull him back, she banged her stick and got back quick. Till the time we realize it was too late. A blink of eye and I see the hurting view of us falling deep like the Earth cracked open.

2

Double Trouble

The only thing I could do was protect spike by throwing him up so he lands on me, but chances were low. I bet he wanted to protect me too, cause he was holding my hand from his pointy tale and trying to chack rocks and wall to save us both. But nothing worked and I had the last glance of my friends, and everything went black. Until Jack Jack wake up, he is breathing, you are fine Jack Jack "Hissss".

I opened my eyes and saw them in cuts and scratches, bleeding red but fine and alive. I was relieved and so were they, and I woke up, we see up some people covered in black were blocking the entrance. The next moment everything was black, I realized now we were on a net with stones all around. Everybody?, what happened?!, It is dark here! Anybody have torch? "hiisss" I heard them screaming. Oh no nobody has torch here we are doomed Logan said. Wait calm down and no moment the rock above us could still fall we have to figure out a way I said. Wait I saw a face other than us it was hers harlow said. Calista are you here with us I asked, and she spoke up terrifying others and me too. Ahhhhh everyone screeched in horror and ran around the place, when a rock falled not so big but enough to make the place bloody. Thankfully nobody was hurt, she told she was up to help them six and jumped to save them which ended up trapping her too. Ok wait thing and remember what that lady told he is to test us, we can't fail otherwise everything is over said Annabelle. Skylar said we need important items which made this idea pop up in Annabelle and my mind. We can use the net as rope as he are not that high from the ground, and we did so. Using stones we all collected the rope after cutting it, we were up for big stripes. Down we all were and were looking like attacked by a pack of wolf. We looked around and found an empty side, meaning something was behind that big plate of rock, it sounded empty. Some brutal damage and the stone plate was in pieces(brutal damage to our hands not the artifical carved plate kept there to make us think it's a dead end.) Brutal damage to the wall too but more of to our hands.

The thing behind the stone thing was Light, white light and there goes this thing. It was a giant maze but instead of plants or stones guarding the place from violating the path, there were mirrors. Which makes it extreamly difficult to get through. We all first tried to make a big joint rope and get out through where they accidently came in. It didn't worked and I doubted the rope to be strong enough. Not having much choice we went ahead with bunch of stones big and small, we carried all we can and maybe you know why! It was originally Skys(skylars pet name) idea to break the mirror to see more wisely and log(logans pet name) updated it by carrying the mirror. He knew they contain silica and metals are used to reflect light. We went ahead getting lost several times, brock many mirrors and did this till we were out of stone stocks. Stones were done and we had alot of mirror pieces. An hour I estimated, it took us to get free from the maze, everybody was quite in the way. Yess we are out Ben screamed, when har warned to not make noise as we have no idea what stands ahead.

After coming out of the tragic maze we see, A large room almost empty, with 5 throne type chaire and stairs at the corners. It was an echoing place. There were chambers, like pathways to a room without a door, there were total 21 of them, meaning we could choose from 21 rooms, where to go. At the center we saw fruits and I was from the one who wanted to go eat it, but I knew some traps can be present, or they were everywhere. The place was sus and we glided some mirror on the wall to check for any trap, nothing happened. We still can't be sure Ana told. When spike ran for the fruit basket and bought it to us without any troble in the way. Quite a shock for me! Log and har are best with fruits and vegetables so thay had a look, then cutted a peice of orange and had a bite. Everything was fine but next one was half rotten, so minimum effort and some time and they have something to munch on. We all shared equally like best friends and were sitting full.

Now we are no more hungry anymore so what should we do sky asked in good mood. We can go in any of the 21 rooms, you'll saw how dark it was said Calista. We sure can but our main motive should be get out of here from the hole that was made when we falling. We can find things that can help us doing that I said and spike helped too. We are seven people so 7 multiplied by 3 har said, you mean one person will go in 3 different dark rooms Sky said. Probably if we can survive the first one Calista added. We have no idea what's behind oh there is no door, what's behind the dark light so we can't separate Ana told. That means we can go in pairs or altogether Log said. What happened Ben asked me! I was looking down and was probably scared and lost, my hope was ending as I was feeling alone when they proved me wrong. So pretty hard right it is right said har. Why scared when we all are still together said log. Yeah you are from the smart people you can't let yourself down said sky. What to be afraid of we have the thing made of sand said ben referring to mirror. I know you are the strongest so make yourself an example said ana. So No need to worry said Calista. Then I said something unexpected "Oh it's not like you think I was worried cause spike didn't have his favorite food!" Yeah it left them kind of speechless and confused maybe. Now the important thing, we are on the edge of a knife, a wrong step and it's all over. So we moved ahead where the basket was and something from above at the straight end open. It was in front of us but we ignored it and now we could see how big of a mistake was it. It got open, some hard mechanism said Calista, and people were coming down from the auto-appearing stair. I would be scared I said seeing them coming down.

Then the next moment they were in front of us, no one from our side moved and was watching curiously. Their number kept increasing, 37 why so many sky said, she ment people. There was one man in specific I was looking, I had a thought that he was behind all of this. Then a man suddenly comes ahead wearing black clothes and even cool glasses and said. Live your last moment, that you decide, use your brain like never before and try to!!! Who are you asked Logan angrily! Then I screamed now and went ahead, punching him hard. Others did what I was doing but with a little more confusion than me. We hurted nearly 10 gaurds, good for 12-year-olds and I was from the very few who took down two. You know what happened next, A bomb blasted and the only thing we could see was nothing, Just joking we all were being hold by gaurds and was going to be taken to a place you will know about. The man I mentioned before, the one looking like the leader came ahead and told what you thought you could win the fight, little brat! On which I replied sorry couldn't hold the spirit of a liger(hybrid of animal and tiger) then had a proper look while the people in black suits were taking us somewhere. In the way I screamed, "Hey, leader guy you know I too got the leadership and loyalty of my new friends!" I expected a good place! I told my old angry friends and just as the gaurds were gone something scared me.

It were my own friends yelling on me, but I had a heart of stone and lion. More than one minute and they were still scolding me, not everyone though. My heart of stone was taking a bath in nitric acid and heart of lion was breaking down. We were in a place made by non-carved stones, it was much of a small place with strong bars blocking our way to freedom. There was just one gaurd for us prisoners and it didn't looked like there was any cameras. So before I could start Annabelle spoke up, she silenced everyone and said. Use your brain It was a clever thing he did, going in any of those 21 room could be anything so his manipulation, he bought us hear! Yep I knew her capabilities and added his main attention is on me and he probably think we are not to much on genius, so we have better chance. I kind of knew you were not doing any stupidity, Sorry sky said, and everyone was up when I told "you know it's kind of lame, so no apologies!" See I never scolded, I mean not that much Calista said.

Moving ahead we had a plan, to make! We knew how the path looked like, we saw when they were bringing us behind the bars. There were rooms, and probably people behind them so what to do??? Some hard thinking and listening to many idea we all have no choice but to agree with ben. His idea, to break the bars so we can escape and what I said an this, "It's so obvious". This time har and Calista upgraded his idea with reference to me, I guess. It was to break the stones where the bars were stuck tight and collect them, knock the gaurd and get back through were we started, after that escape from the top with the help of the bars. Ana know this would not work, me too.

The thing we just can't escape with only some metal bars! Anyways everybody decided to do this at night, like we knew what time is it. We have some time to modify our ideas! We were just sitting down quite and talking to each other in pair, no real group talk happened except one when sky told us about a possible danger maybe and I replied quite well, it was looking depressing.

Some time and we were up for the dangerous plan. when I told can anyone take care of spike and everyone was up except logan. So I said girls you have it, please take care cause some people are afraid. Now it was the time we started to break free the bars by breaking the stones by the stones we have cause they took our mirror pieces. It took us longer than we thought but it was coming up. One side we broke and the bottom remains, we broke that to and the we have 6 bars not so big.

Now we came in front of the gaurd and said now your turn!!! Are you serious! Don't you know this much noise would definately grab anyones attention. You expect you would live after that! "I smiled a little," then he said, go! now's the time!, there should be nobody up run straight through! The things you told before, Do you think I don't know about it already. Then we ran and Ben said we will meet again, I hope. We were in the mirror maze when har had a thought to use the mirrors to climb. It was not that useful but this made an idea pop in ana's mind, it was. To use the board behind the mirror! She ment the mirrors were attached to a wooden board and we can use it to climb up somehow. We were up for it and broke many of them, it sure was hard at first but it got easier when we figured out the proper way. we had many of it and then we reached the beginning and were killed after what we saw. The way from where we came was filled with cement. After we came here they would have done it blocking the entrance with cement, they would have done the same thing above from where we fell. It was all about time and they arrived(the people who captured us). We are here to an dead end Calista said slowly without any feelings. They captured us and said Be Ready before covering our face with a cloth bag!

They took us somewhere and threw us all in a vehicle I took a peice of mirror secretly, we were in with it's door locked up closed and no light. It was quite, no one said a word and it was freaking me out. I am scared of dark and silence too and both combined... I asked, you all with me? while searching for someone. Yeah we with you I recognised him from his voice, it was Ben. And I also found someone, I asked who are you and she repliedI am Harlow, Jack you are scared aren't you. No worries we all are close by she said, good thing we can touch to know but our hands are still tied up I said. Anything anyone has to say asked Calista. Is it is!? said log, Don't forget we all are still together! said sky. Yeah, we will be alright, maybe people are searching for us said har. Something we left behind! told Benjamin. Don't forget me! told Calista, and We don't ever give up! said Ana. She stole my line, I was like, but I said harder. So think everybody we have to hunt our freedom, said ben, find is a better word sky said. It would be dark outside I let everyone know. We can't do anything, just wait said Calista, and we did so. The door got opened and everybody was asleep on the way except for me and ana we were trying to figure out the distance. But now as the door is open we see, nothing cause our hands and legs were tied up by a rope and a blindfold was on. They took us somewhere and opened our blindfold and the ropes.

We see tons of trampolines, a play zone to complete some task for fun and many more, it was like we are enjoying our holidays. It was suspicious though, they let us in and were told to play whatever we want in here. There was one thing, spike was missing!!! Well we had a good look and found nothing dangerous. So we were up bouncing for hours completing challenges with no disturbance and a lot of food and water. We enjoyed for hours maybe 4 or more and then eat alot and played more, it was when log noticed something suspicious and let us know. Then we wasn't able to hold ourself and slept, I mean, you will know! We woke up knowing many things and found out we are not where we were. It was a room small and blank with nothing but white walls and a door, it was where we woke up. Ana went ahead and opened the door and we were glad to see, A thing that looked like an escape room.

The thing we saw was something more scary, there were postures of horror movies and bloody terrifying postures everyone. There were some depressing ones too! We too saw all sorts of things and messy and dirty walls, which looked overfilled. Carpets were spread down and things were hanging, things like light and a small working fan. There was a lot to figure out but this question was in my mind, which I said out loud. How the heck were we bought here???

We had a plan, you can say I had a plan or no, stick around with we. It was for Ben to search behind the scary postures cause I was afraid. Logan was for the things hanging up and then the carpet below. Har was for the objects all around cause she was the best in finding things.

Then I choosed to search the white blank room but still was afraid to do it alone so ana suggested calista to help me. But I took sky with me and told calista to search the other walls. As ana was helping others. There were 2 cupboard-Wardrobe thing with many columns in this with two "L" paths going through the "I" line starting from the white wall room to the path distribution. I took a vessel and broke it on the white wall and it happens to be a good thing. We found nothing for the wall and I said whatever you find keep it to you until we have our next meeting. We were finding the wall when she told, glad to be alive but why are they doing this? A question I have no answer! we sure will know if they don't kill us, or us ourselves.

Floor checked, wall check and the top remains only for us, she being a little taller than me was taking advantage of finding nothing. Yeah we found nothing even after doing dozens of tests. I took a step out and down there I found it, a broken peice of the vessel, it looked sus so I picked it up. And something was a very tiny bit out from corner with different color. It barely catched it and peeled it off, It was a sticker, a blank sticker. Not yet over it was, it still looked sus, and I knew it, it was just a sticker on a sticker. So I peeled off the sticker which was on the sticker, which was hard and found this thing. "* * *", there were 3 small diamonds made, which looked like asterisks. I was glad from many things now, first it's stickiness was alot and never-ending, second the sticker on the sticker was much more like a matte paper and the sticker it was on was like a glossy paper with that printed. As you can expect they found 2 things behind the postures and were having a perfect look to see for any clue in the postures. There were 2 Cupboard-Wardrobe thing at the ending of the room, and when we shift them we see doors at both the sides. In one Cupboard-

Wardrobe thing there was a box with a lock, stronger than anyone I know and in other Cupboard-Wardrobe thing a box which can oly be opened with the passcode. Other than that we see nothing in any of the 2 Cupboard-Wardrobe things. I was searching for more things other than what my friends discovered, when ana stops me. She asked me about the light, it had something more which made it sus. I checked it and knew it instantly, it was a capacitor. I broke the glass and detached the capacitor from the metal rod not at all affecting the light, which indicates the light and electricity system is customised by them. It although stopped the small fan, I said "We might just have discovered something accidently!" Everybody gathered and then we shared our discoveries. Some discoveries you didn't knew about:- First off from beneath the carpet, there was a big layer of cotton, and beneath the cotton layer we see a leather layer and beneathe that a perfect circle.

There was a metal box there which left almost no gap fitting in the circle. The box was heavy and no portion of it came out. Second at a corner at the top, it sound empty and after breaking the perfectly fitted wood we found a giant battery. There too was a big magnet with a handle. We knew just the thing, so with the help of the powerful magnet Logan the strongest pulled up the metal box. Which could further be opened, after opening it we found, A torch, a powerful electronic torch. Third thing was a key sky spotted in one of the postures. Forth the inside the frame of the only opened door, inside the wood we found it the key Now some more and there we are!

3

Escape room

We inserted the battery and turned on the light and flashed it all over then after a minute off the torch and found this right above our head. It read "The key you have, for one to choose, Beware, the wrong one makes you lose!" What did we missed said cal! The table were the vessel was kept on, that table had it, I mean the three cool looking sticks holding it up. We checked everywhere, where can it be ben asked on which I replied, we didn't searched ourselves! It seems out this was a very useful advice cause each of us found a key small but the key for the lock. We bought it together and it sticked, which concludes it to be a magnet. Then we opened our first key opening lock and found a grenade, a real grenade! Why is this here! asked ben. To blast of something ,what can you think replied ana. Sky, har, and log were scratching the wall with the sticks for fun, with they tore the wallpaper. We took it off and saw something, there was something written!

Screw
er ehk cits
un door

It was like this! What do you think we can conclude, three different language, creators of this went crazy, or use our brain to figure out. I somehow still had that peice of mirror! And that's all we need, A mirror in front of the words. Read it backwards and it spells stick here if you read properly. The glossy paper right on the backwards *stick here* and nerds get it. That diamond asterisk is used as separators in books it was spot by ben, he is not a nerd but he pays attention on everything except you already know. So just to remove the screw from the first door, as un in french is one which can be concluded for 1st, french was a famous language. We didn't have any screw driver, I went ahead to have a closer look and found the number 4875 written on the screws of the door. I got the number and it was just the passcode of the other box. What we find a box full of diamonds, everyone was happy except for me, trying to figure out what is going on. We then flashed the powerful light on both the doors cause we couldn't find screwdriver. Then it appeard it spelled "A lion who hasn't eaten a fresh human from 3 years" on the first door. And on second "The holy lava from the legend of the island with the sacred volcano, kept preserved for years to kill" a peice of cake. I and ana picked up the second option and others the first, but seeing us the switch. The I said the lava is already cool and solid, that's when they understood. We left the first door and broke the second one, and we were there no lava but a clear path. We walked with a sharp view and then opened the door in front of us, when we were at the end.

While we were walking Calista asked isn't the lion dead, on which ana replied maybe cause it can still eat animal flesh!!! We opened the door and see gaming computers with a lot of food and gaurds. They instructed us to eat/drink and complete the 10 minecraft challenges in 10 hours. We have to think and escape the challenges ahead. 10 challenges 10 hours and they were off! Just 4 hours maybe and it was all done, I mean we played minecraft for hours everyday! The challenges was up now so what! the answer, we go to sleep. They gave us bed and when we were awake we find ourselves. In a biiiiig room, a hall maybe, but we were not alone. There were a thousand dogs all around us, ok little bit more than 300 only. They were running all around when har asked what is going on? That's what we have to figure out ana replied! Then there from above they dropped a ton of food everywhere. We were standing still even though it was hard. Log said id there anybody who hate dogs, Nope everybody replied by moving their head. So why are they here har asked, maybe a little rest after this much effort cal said.

The number of dog kept increasing and soon the room started to look small! Just standing there and looking at the dogs having no idea what to do, something scared me! well, all of us. The dogs were fighting over for food and we were standing in their hive, that means we were to be attacked by hungry dogs. Well I listened, "I hungry man is always an Angry man", now I'm seeing it said said har. Just so you know, the wildness multiplies with dogs! said ana. So now what ~log. The top there's a window!, if we can climb up we would be safe up there. There was a big circle, no oval shaped window but it was in covered in black paint with little to none light to be seen. But how we all are gonna reach up there asked ana! Yeah that's some height calista told. Believe me if we all together, helping each other out, we can do it! I told. We were there standing just below the window when I said. So now what to do...

There's a small slap right on my head by har and everybody got angry. Yeah, I was just joking I told them.

Then my plan log and ben on the ground, har and sky on top of them and I on top of them. Ana and cal wait! We took some tries but within a minute we made our human structure, well a minute or 3, maybe more. There I reached the windows wooden cover, which was all around the window giving a place to sit or clean. There I told ana and cal to climb up and then pulled them over, then I and others helped sky and har to get up here. Now the challenging part how to get ben and log up, to make it even harder the dogs were trying bite them now. We got to do something quick said sky. Then I told the girls to hold my legs and I with my hand will pull them up. Now you know I said together we can do anything! On fails and it's all over. We executed the plan and I was hanging up-side-down. I catched bens hand and log was holding ben tight so I can pull them both up. Up the girls were trying their best and down they were hanging trying the dogs to not cath them and in between me, who was stretching my height and keeping me up by some motivational quotes by unknow motivator artist, which was maybe myself. It was a lot of weight and I was to give up when log did this. He jumped from ben to me and then up to the window resting place. We were almost there when he did this, his move made me give off and my hand was slipping off Ben. It was that time when I knew, wait log...

He would have jumped holding the wooden thing with hands, cause I saw his legs hanging down. He instructed ben to hold his leg and leave my hand, Don't worry he said me and did what log told him to do. He was strong enough to pull him and ben together up, I was almost fainted and my body was loose. But my friends pulled me up and I was up! I then standing, well sitting, umm both together was in front of them all when ben said, looks like we did it! All thanks to everybody I said. Not yet cal said in the conversation and what happened now was everybody reaction. She said what about the disgusting smell! What can you expect dog poop everywhere. We sat there for some minutes maybe almost an hour when har realized, "The window". We can break it and be free, great idea ana said but a little risky. They didn't wasted a minute though and were already trying to break the glass down. I said the glass could be bulletproof, they had wasted so much of money doing these things why not spend on this too. They ignored and glad to know, I was wrong, the glass got a crack. I anyways was trying to scratch the color of the window. Some more time and they would break the thing it looked like, and I could see it light. I scratched some more and was up making a plan to really escape the place. It looked like we were on third floor or higher and there was this big and wide building we were in. There was another building in front of this one, a part of this building cause it was connected making a "U" shape.

We are almost there I heard by log, I called them to have a look outside and when they were I did this. I came there where they were breaking the window and with full power completed their task. It was a big hole we made, I also grabbed their attention. Then, I said look after me and jumped down and landed on a not so big place looking like a balcony with no entrance. however just beside where I landed there were some paint boxes and other minor stuff, but the thing that I came down for was a rope. I saw it from up, then grabbed it and threw it up tell them to catch it, there was another one and I wrapped it around my body. I had a feeling somebody is watching me so I hurried. They were holding it strong and I quickly climbed up. Once I was up with the other rope I told them. "Be ready". There was a pole on the building attached horizontally to the building. I threw a rope from the pole hanging down and instructed everyone the hold the rope they are tight and strong, then I jumped for the rope and catched the hanging side of the rope and told them to pull the rope slowly. They till now were little bit shocked but it is normal for me! I was now sitting on the pole. From there I jumped to another pole asked for the other rope and tied three knots on a corner. The rope being fat was enough to be stuck in a gap between the metal pipe, of course after many tries. I dared to climb up the rope and seconds later was standing on top of the building. From there I told log to climb up easy while I hold the rope above him. He climbed up and it was heavy enough, but now we can help everyone climb the rope like log without doing any hard pole jumping.

We were currently standing on the terrace(top of the building), finding cables or path to the other side for an easy escape. We were in middle of the jungle, just a big fat area with some land free otherwise everywhere you first see, it is green. Everybody choosed the long way to the other side but I saw a bunch of cables connecting the other side. Can't help that it's in my nature, also I was there faster than others. So some waiting and exploring with eyes I had a plan to escape.

What is it to connect the rope and with it's help come down to the soil. We just ran into the woods, we were afraid to be caught. We ran some minutes but out of nowhere they catched us. Captured us and again but in their van, to a short ride back to the building. Our face was covered in black bags and one more thing if you think I left spike, not at all! There is no chance they would kill him and we with a armed government authorities raid on them. We from the room we escaped we going to another room when they let us see the destruction we escaped. Even the windom was destroyed, it was slow but it was evil. Congrats you officially solved the third task! a man said after we entered the next room. What? Who are you? we asked questions like this. He with loud voice stopped us telling "you will know!" He then told, "Dog treat" the third tasks name, was a surprising one, so sorry you missed it, but don't you worry it wont happened again he said on logs face. Ben pushed him away asking do any of other you call task have name? What do you think! Escape room for the first, MIFT for the second, you already know the third, and "Creepy crawls" the forth one. It shall be easy for mud brains like you! he said and darkened the room. A minute later the lights were up filling the whole of the room. Now we see, there is nothing, nothing at all said log. Are you sure? A voice said from the mic somewhere in the room. We could see some cams spying on us, a plain room with white and light blue colour. We saw many tables but now they were all gone! There were just cups like a normal cup but wider. The voice from the mic instructed us to take one cup for each. We moved ahead and did what it said, two cups remains huh said calista.

The the voice said what we have to do. It said there are 6 small but poisonous! Catch them and beware of a minute, it multiples. What! It just left us scared! said sky and har. Yeah girls are scared of lizards, right! we teased. Then, a long loud scream and we all screamed on the scream too. What happened asked ben, ana replied I turned behind and see this a big fat lizard crawling right behind mee! We looked behind and... Big? Fat? said ben and log, That is like not even half a foot, and see its belly that is fat??? they teased more.

4

The crawling hunt

Well, at least I was quite. We were spotting more lizards now when, something scared me. An siren type noise, the lights in the room turned red and were blinking. It blinked 3 times and everything was fine again. What was that asked cal, Ahhhhhhh! I screamed cause the lizard was near my leg. You could have catched it said ben, it took me time to realize but I did. Guess boys are scared more they teased.

After 2 minutes of serious lizard hunting we found out that there are more than 6 lizard in the big room, we were also tired of the red alarm siren playing every minute. I was smart enough to encode the meaning of what it said on mic. Every minute they increase the number of lizard and gave the red siren three times. Ok so first we have to shut down the way from where the wizard were coming I said. We looked down and saw we could slide their entrance place, which was a small panel connected to somewhere. We did and it was smaller, small enough to stop them. It wors like this, there were some gaps in the metal double metal plate located down at the wall. And if we slide one we make the gaps smaller, which is small enough to stp them. Looks like planned! Now what should we do with the left of the free lizards! ana said. On which I replied "It's time to bring the old friend back!" What are you talking about they reacted. See this! I said don't worry anybody caus spike is back. I with excitement raised my hand and here he comes from the sleeves. Everyone pet him and asked how?! Well someone helped I told while playing a bit.

Then I told him "go buddy show how deadly can the 15th deadliest snake can be!!!" He went for it and I followed, everyone to and then I told him only kill. He agreed 'sadly' and went for it, it's all about time and we were done with the task. But they cheated! They announced to look at the floor cause what you see wuld be hard to digest! Guess what we see down, and hundred of cockroaches all around. Oh no there are more thousands coming I said, Surely everybody freaked out. Spike was around my neck and my brain was just not working. What can we do! har asked, so intelligent they have no window here sky said. So I have nothing more to do, I thought! I looked at everyone and said it's going to be sharp! Then looked at a camera and screamed "I know the Invader!" The voice over the mic said "Jump!" and we did almost at the perfect time. The plate with a sharp edge was released, it filled the entire room and killed all the cockroaches. I turned to my friends and told them to "use your brain like never before!" We couldn't be able to defeat them physically but we can with our mental powers "There is a war ahead my friends," and you will win if you follow what I said. Ok not so dense "I always wanted to say that!" and yeah I still believed we can defeat them in a fight.

The gaurds with a new head man I never say came in, I was ready. He came to me punched me on my face hard and ordered the gaurds to hold my friends. He hold me from my T-Shirt, my mind was feeling dizzy but I tried to control.

He was taking me somewhere forcefully and I started to tell everything I can to my friend in my way. I told them, "Be brave and in your mind, find clues be together, make yourself worth-y for every-one. They are testing us, we shall pass, use everything you can!" Then I told the gaurds and everyone "I told all my friends a thing a clue you have to find, they are coming and my friends hold the knowledge in parts other than me!" My last thing to my friends "Take care of him!!!" The guy carrying me punched me again and took me to a room, his punch really hurts, I was probably tired and could not feel thing anymore but my part of brain was working fine and that's all that matters. They threw me in a room, just a table, and 2 chairs. On one sat a person strong and manipulative, and on other me. I sat down and tried to relax when he asked "feeling like a prisoner."

I knew what to do, I was quite and inspecting, like he was. So tell me you both teamed up, maybe to escape a low security prison he said. Why don't you beat me up and throw me in a little higher security prison! I said. Oh sure but just one thing I want to know, so tell me he forced holding my chin. There are many stronger than your gaurd, they are everywhere, even one of your most trusted person. Do you know why? I knew this, so my friends I told them the important information other than me. They have power and armed weapon, they're quantity is more some time and you lose I said. You will see who loses! he said with agitation. Then stood up and told me to tell me everything I knew, I refused and said him beat me hard it doesn't hurt after the torture. And, He did punched me hard on the face, I was however still up, he punched me more but I was not to quit. Until that last punch, it hit me hard, harder and I was down on the floor and I said "he told me during your weak prison hold cause I am more than just a normal boy!"

So now kill me fast cause that is better than you use me for evil! I said in serious dizziness and almost in unconsciousness, well I was feeling like that. He came to me hold me by hair and said "oh I will," I smiled when he punched me hard right on the face, and I can't think, a gap in time.

My eyes got opened and I was at height, a waterfall, on a cliff, tied with ropes, with many gaurds and the bosses present. They looked at me and said "sad to loose a smart person, you could have done a great job in your future but you choosed the hard way." You still have a chance, tell us! one of the boss said. (note there are several bosses but one 3 heads and a main!) Never! Are you sure you can kill me cause I see my people here they are within you all I said. I was on the edge and when they looked behind I jumped right in the waterfall and of course survived. I knew how to jump from heighs in water, saw many self safety tutorial. Ahead I see another waterfall sucking me, a bunch on crocodile on the ground and a lot of sharp rocks in the water. At this time I knew it was luck most of and why was I here, "there is no chance of surviving also with hands tight." I used every bit of my strength and walked in the high stream of water, it was hard so hard I could feel myself like never before. I was to an edge and hoped up, it was the right side and the crocodiles were on the left. It looked a path created to trap me if I survive. I could see an apple tree and I went for it, my power was almost over and I needed food to gain my strength back. The apples were high for my height and I lay down seeing the apple hoping it to fall. My eyes were closing and I saw helicopters flying over, it was the last thing I saw.

∞∞∞

"Huuuhhh" I exhaled long and some deep breathing and I was back, I stood up climbed the tree got many apples and was looking fine. I thought it was over but no, I have to go save my friends I said. I can go to the authorities or handle it myself, and I went for the second option. I knew where my friends were(that building) so I after eating some apples and carrying some ran for it. It took a long time but not at all long if you see because it was dark and I got scared. Reaching there I saw the view and knew what to do, there were cameras everywhere and open entrances. I knew where the cameras were not, cause of the escape before, so from the portion of the building I climbed up. I too knew the terrace was not that strong for the same reason as before(escape). So once I was up the terrace I tried to ear for my friends from the floor. The thing there were no gaurds up, and the building had no visitor but still has full electric and power supply, this was odd. I had the rope we left from before and I located my friends, so what to do now? Break the floor and have a heroic entry, "Easier said than done." There were some bricks and here I started to breck the floor. Down everybody could hear the sound and I decided to run! not for what you think. I was successful in that and settled not far from the building. I planned to be captured cause till now I would have done a big thing disturbing their plan. But we all could be killed in it, so I make weapons to help. It was morning and I survived. I found many things thrown away by the people in the building things like pan, stove, bowl, clothes, and many more. I went for a little exploration round to get an idea to make a weapon. I was looking for things when I found blue flowers, and attached to it flax seeds. I had the perfect idea. To use the containers left behind by them and the flax seeds I found and make "linseed oil" an oil which can catch fire without a spark. I planned to make a lot and lot of it to burn down their building. How to make linseed oil? simple mix 2 tablespoon of water with 10 to 20g of flax seed while the water boils. I went ahead and collected a lot of seed, really it was a lot, then used the big kitchenry, there were a lot of metal left by them and made fire from the woods which exhausted me, Then after some failed attempt made a lots of oil to burn then down. I also took my time to fill my stomach. Then made many rough tools from wood and random stones, it was like a 50 tools and place it to the opposite side from where I enter the top of the building. I left a lot of fruit to and then times for the hard task, "cover the build with the oil." I had a lot of leaves which I spread everywhere and then by little-little applied the oil. It really takes a nerve to do it and a lot of time too. In the way finding resources I found red shiso and sorrel, mix it together and you have fake blood. I had some oil and with leaves climbed up, found the bricks and started to break the floor. I was close to break it when I covered my self in fake blood, if real wasn't enough. Then with full power I breck it, I could see them "my friend", so I dropped all the leaves I had then on it all the linseed oil. I attached the rope to a circular antenna and slowly came down shocking my friends. As I expected there were no gaurds, cause my friends were in full security prison and the tools, food and fire I left there, "yes" had the gaurds attention. I told my friends to climb up with me fast and they did. Up on the terrace everybody hugged me and some talks like they told us you were dead and you know the reply "I can't die so easy!" But then I rushed down with my friends and ran, they surely knew we were escaping but the thing that stopped them from coming after us was "their building was on fire!!!"

How did you do that? everybody asked and I said them everything. But it is not over yet we have to run I said. We were at a distance know when behind we see The 2 bosses with gaurds stopping our escape. They captured us and bought us back to their headquarters, the building was off fire, they controlled it and stopped it spread further away. Then I heard a voice, my and others face was covered. It said "Glad to see you alive!" Now for your 5th task you got to seperate! Just after him saying this the gaurds forcefully carried us to our small different rooms. It was of a size of a living room, and the only thing I had to to was to survive. I will be given no food, no water, no help, no electricity, no nothing. They told me this and left me to myself, they also told meet you after 3 days. I know just the thing to do! Break the cameras, and I did so, But then a voice from the mic said "we have those everywhere!" and I decided to live like normal.

∞∞∞

The first day and I already start seeing mouses send by them, I was alright after all I am used to it. The thing that I did was I imagined a better universe, I thought of the possibilities that lies in the multiverse ahead and did my own thought experiment. I although was worried for my friends!

It was the 2nd day without food and water, there was a toilet although but water was non. The mouse was a serious problem, nah not for me, I made them my friend, 'white rat'. It was the 3rd day and I was really starving now, I drank a little liquid but my tongue was almost dead. I waited, there was nothing else to do, I was really suffering now which made me worried. If I am like this what about my friends! It was time 2 people came in and had lots of food and water with them, they also bough a soft drink. They were leaving when one gaurd said "you almost got us there, also gain all the knowledge about survival cause the last 2 are going to be deadlier than ever. They left taking all the mouse and I had a nice launch to eat, just I didn't know that it's a launch or dinner or in between. Anyways I ate a lot and was feeling better now but I still didn't knew why I was in the bedroom prison. Surprising thing it has been another day time passes slow and there is nothing much to do. I had no idea what to do, just spending time in hunger and depression. I gave a thought on how the outside world and my mom would be doing, cause no FBI has opened up.

∞∞∞

My eyes opened, I slept while thinking and now I see, nothing. They transported me to another room in my sleep and I had a black bag on. My hands were free so do my legs , I was also on a bed I felt, so there is no reason not to get free of the darkness.

5

Wild to win

The darkness is out and now I see. Sitting in front of a big screen, in a big white room with less cameras and the sound of rain. I was happy to see them after a long time, they were on the screen, my friends, I could hear them. There was no gaurd in the big room, just screen, faces and their sound. We talked a bit asking about each other like about me she asked the fear of darkness did it got the best of you and I replied I never thought about it, I was fine. We talked for some time desperate to meet when they showed up the gaurds, there were 2 in each of our rooms. One of them said congrats on surviving the "Soundless torture" but ahead lies something not so usual.

The other gaurd said "we arn't their gaurds," tell me what do you know about me time is running. What! I reacted. Ok kid we mean no harm the other one said we are here to destroy their plans and same you all and the others. I said I don't know about you'll I knew something was fishy so I used the doubtful situation to my freedom. They looked little stun and told me everything. They said "Hey, kid listen there are many more groups of children here and the mastermind of this tasks ambitions isn't good!" There are

17 of us in their building to let you all free, see there your friends are knowing this all too. You mostly have to solve a couple party games like others did but if there is something else, you know the head is taking serious intrest in your group. We gotta go now be safe and if you survive you will be up for "The Seventh Task" Be good. They said and left I figured out the cameras were off in the time, I starred at them while I was in the bedroom prison. Hahahahaha! A laughter we heard. Then a man suddenly enters our call, cam off mic on he said. Be ready you are going to meet each other soon, (everybody was happy and excited) but then he said "In the middle of Ocean!" he left the call.

We waited in horror not one said a word online, just thinking what they want us to do. Some minutes later some gaurds came in my room, one as recognizable. I had a plan and I said it to him, I also told him some tricks of science to win the fight. They had us now all together in different boats heading to a ship. I got it now I was unconscious for a day and when woke up we all were already far away from each other, that means they did something with us in the time we were down. I in the boat told a gaurd "Your leaders are cowards to not see us yet!" and he replied "You will be glad to see them there!" Ok we are to die a painful death I thought but my rationality was in my control. I was kinda worried watching the ocean and how it moves but then I have my friends. I was ready! I see a big ship half the size of titanic in the ocean and we have arrived. The gaurds took me all the way to a floor, I forgot the count in the way. There the door opened and I say them, two more doors. After some door opening I open the magic door and *exhales. Nice to see you I say and they came to me for a nice hug. We have time now It was night till the time I reached and we talked a lot like never before. They gave us food, dinner I suppose and we were still gossiping. Until it was time for bed, we had our nice comfy beds and I felt a good morning ahead waits. We woke up did what a normal person does for the one last time and 8AM it was, we were standing in front of 3 people the one who manage everything and the one mastermind behind the idea of these games more likely tasks. When are you gonna kill us! I asked just the moment we meet.

He replied oh not me we have more than hundreds of sea creatures ready in the ocean water ahead, you got to survive an island if that doesn't kills you. How many more you have killed ana asked the number goes in hundreds he replied. And why are you doing this asked har You don't need to know he replied utterly. We will shock you by surviving the ocean and the seventh task, just see Ben said to him. You will return home then it has been a decade seeing them he replied again. When are you gonna throw us open in the water cal asked, you'll have a boat and more he said. Anything you wanna say! Why you did this? asked log, oh there is no need he replied agitatedly. He then came to us had a glare and gave his command for us to get in the boat at a distance then never to be seen again. While going sky told him "I will call you roadroller!" and I said I hope you are destroyed. There we set off never to be seen again, there were just the seven of us on board. The creature we see were amazing, they reminded me of spike I had him to stay with one of the fake gaurd. There were sharks, octopus, small fishes and more, they were swimming close, I saw spears, some sticks basically weapons. Ben, log, har, sky and ana too, they picked up the weapons. That is when I knew, what sky calls "roadroller's" intension, he wants us to attack the inocent creatures. Yeah, inocent because they were basking sharks and whale sharks, they mean no harm to humans. I identified one of the octopus which was Bimac Octopus, most friendly octopus by far I know.

It was clear they want us to attack them but that's wrong. I told my friends to drop the things and we kept on sailing, we were seeing them(sea creature) mind there own business. I told them everything I thought about the situation and tried to remember everything I learned from survival videos and books. Looks like I am not so dumb as I was shown in the beginning of the story! We all sat down, there was some food given by them evil people and we have to save it in order to survive. The weather was bad not worse at least, we were ready to live the worst of natures crises. And guess what happened we all slept, I suppose that was a good decision cause when we woke up the weather was nice. Talk about surviving something like this, there still was just water till far away. I was telling my friends a story about an island rather bit of magical and mysterious, it was the legend of nekros lieweg. We all talked for entertainment and it waas time 3 hour has passed and we can see an island now. Don't know if it was a real island cause it was barely 400m long. My first step on the island followed by my friends and "it's going to be hard here!" I said.

Don't worry a reply from back. Ok so you are the boss what to do asked log, Let's see they have came to this island before and may have left something. But we have to find water, food and shelter or make one for ourself I replied. Let's become caveman now said ben, nah we possess knowledge and skills, we will become rulers said ana. Yeah lets do it a cheerful quote by sky and we start. Little description about the small island, I would call home. It has got a lot of trees, stones and the ground has dirt not just sand. There are also many types of trees and plant and resources like materials. It clears one thing many things were upgraded and added to this island by roadrollers guys. It had what a normal island have and it completely makes sense to test us in the form of using scratch. So happy to watch dr.stone!!! We discussed about some important things like not to ignore any signs of any of us from close or far. Coordinate, use everything we can find, and give it our all cause we a super smart. So first thing we do is gather woods, log, cal and sky are going to do that. Then ben you have to make fire with sticks cause you once told me you know many ways to make fire. I, har and ana are going to find a place, a perfect shelter and maybe a river stream type thing. Got it everybody I asked and we set off after a cheerful "Yea", ana told we meet hear again.

We do the work we decide and hour passes. We found many good places but not like the one that was the best, and har having experience in hiking and all those camping stuff was our leader. 2 hours in the island and we have found a good place to stay, many many woods. Ana and har stay to the place we found and I went to guide everyone to there. I reach there and see ben alone, there were sticks down and I thought he wasn't able to make fire and told let's try again. But he told "Not just you me too come in the category of science, smarty!" We have a boat full of supplies including water bottles he said. You made fire from water bottles as glass! I asked and his smile gave the answer. We see behind and sky, cal and log came with a lot of woods, I was right they are the strongest of us! We have it now I carry fire and some important stuff from the boat and others carry woods which were more that I saw first. I showed them the way and matter of half an hour we were there. The place we selected was a cave covered, it had some room inside and the entrance was well covered, the was a natural source of water not far from there.

We made the place better burned some woods and drank some water, there was this music going on in my head, it was from a series which describes our situation. We all then gathered some leaves and used them as beds. We ha some food left and ate that as dinner, time was passing we were seeing the stars it looked like time is passing fast. We slept the night and now we are awake thinking of a plan. Har and sky were finding beautiful things as their hobby and some fun. Log and ben were preparing themselves for dangerous situation by punching on trees and some more things like that. Ana and cal were talking to improve the thing we call home. I knew waked up last and the first thing I did was I ran. I ran in full speed to the boat saying them I will be back! I know log would be saying me not obeying my rules. I reached to the boat and was glad to find it missing. There was no sign of it and I was upset but then I found many torches, all our torch were left down, there was 11 of them. Don't ask me i didn't packed our 'Boat'. I carried them back and said this after meeting them. Our only plan is to escape this island! 'huh' they reacted, how can we asked ana. I know, that is why I bought a map of where we are and with it's help we can locate the nearest urban city or town. You sure we can do that? asked cal. If we work together we can I replied.

So go we are with you together said log. I said the "We will do it quick, we will escape this island and complete the seventh task!" Yeah everybody cheered which I didn't expected them to but now it begins, like it already did not. So there are thousands of creatures if not millions that will try to kill us, so keep your uniform dress clean. The nearest peice of hope is little more than 11km away and I don't know it's name, "in fact netheir of us knew!" We can make a steam engine and make a boat from woods covering it in wax and sail our way to never come hear again.

Why don't we make smoke signals and wait for someone to come save us? sky asked, cause no one will, they are still keeping an eye on us, I know. And if that is the case, they think we can escape and you bet we will I said. You know they said survive 30 days on this island and you will be saved ben said. I replied by saying "we can't trust them for our freedom, and suffering here to death is not an option!" So we escape. We run from the challenge said har. There is nothing like challenges, we are there to destroy them. This is the ocean you all, it is dangerous even, so we have to oversmart it with the help of science. I thought I wasted these many years but I forgot to mention how much I studied and now is the ultimate test. It's a big set of wires jumbled together and we have to solve it right asked ana. No! the wires is not what we have to manage, we will ignore it and focus on the things around it and make our escape I replied. Sounds pretty confusing ben said. I have many ideas to make a boat but let me think more wisely, I would recommend you the same thing. So let's start the work now! now! they reacted(not all at least), I said "we are making a boat!" so we would need ropes of different size so... and they interrupted me saying "we already have one." Oh that one, that went away somewhere in the ocean. What! we forgot to tie it to a strong object and it went away with all the stuff inside I said.

They were sure speechless and 5 minutes later after a lot of explaining and convincing we can from where we started. So we need rope and to get that we use... again stopped me and said we can get small thread from leaves and by joining many we make ropes! They ran to gather big leaves and I said bring big leaves. Yeah that annoying moment when one say to do that we already are going to do but it didn't affected them, I heard a OK! So what should I do I asked myself, I just know the thing. Some hour of work going place to place finding and making what we need and at the end of the day it was all worth it. It was more than 9PM we could guess by looking at the sky and we were making food, yeah we collected some to cook at the end of the day. Dinners ready we three said and now we all munch, we were talking and sharing thoughts. We talked a lot and it came to the end by saying we have to work double hard for a week I predict and we are all set and ready to go. Some tired face I said and after some time we are to sleep.

New day we woke up early than yesterday and up to work, "I think it's time for a time-laps!" but how can I miss all the fun, great experience and time, helping and stuff, with the taste of adventure and togetherness we had. Here we are after a week and 5 days later a cool small but big boat in front of made by non other than me, us they corrected. Everybody was kind of sus on me cause I won't lie to you I was making a thing for myself and they don't know about it. You know what it is, okay I can't hide it's a cycle boat...

∞∞∞

Hey hey what to know how we build these boat and ship one by all and other by me only. First the small ship: we found clay in the water and made a strong tools and swords thought we would need them. Then it was to the wood, to carve it in different size and shape. Then to stick we found some metal ores and by melting and shaping it we made nails by bigger. We used sticky liquid from the trees and plants too then the leaves instead of clothes. Don't know why but we tried to froze honey we extracted which didn't worked so we applied it directly. We did a lot of things more and had some things like paddles and were all set to go. Then the cycle boat I made, it has the same mechanism like cycle the tiers have artificial fins to power up like paddle. I made a boat and the cycle thing which had ropes instead of chains. But the gear thing around which the chains I mean ropes revolve was a circle made from wood and had boundaries at left and right. It had pedals and a place which my hands could use to balance and thats all it needs. I attached it to the center of the boat I made, it was small but had enough space and I was ready to go.

∞∞∞

It was time they said "Lets go", we will miss the island and things like that. I, with courage and determination stepped ahead and told them. "You will find ships when you successfully cover the distance of 3km. Be safe cause I have to go from where it all started. It is not more than 4km away I beleive and I have a boat I made! So happy journey I had to get back spike, he is waiting." I told and ran to the cycle boat I made when they stopped me and told we know! how long could you hide and you know what we are coming together. You only said we have to destroy there plans, so lets have a race to their ship and then headquarters. Oh no it maybe already destroyed, I shared a plan according to which at this time they would be fight for the right, you know the friendly gaurds there are hundred more so if my plan goes right and their own modification we win and they lose. What is the plan? ana asked, I know you want to come with me cause you are not stopping me but if the plan doesn't goes the way it should we die!!! Fine! everybody said one by one, I was shocked and they said "we all started together it will end the same way!" I was I, I wasn't able to control the feeling so 'I danced'. No exactly of that but because I was happy and couldn't hold to stop and stand there. We left the next minute. I said out loud "So we have survived everything yet, and this is what that decides our and many others future!" my friends were there for me behind and I was not scared even when a shark passed from near us. I turned back and said "If it doesn't goes the way it should, we fight!" they agreed and we sailed. By the way I was on my cycle boat and they were on the mini ship and I lead the way. it was some hours journey more than I expected, it was morning too.

∞∞∞

We are there we see the ship from a distance now and there we see them captured now by the authorities and the people we met before. We were happy to reach now, there were ropes coming down and we used that to climb up. There we found the person who looked like a inspector telling us to find a safe place cause there were bad people free and running for safety. they would not mind hurting. We found a safe place as the inspector runs to catch them. We were sitting when I saw 4 bad guys hurting one of the guys from our team, I mean a good guy... I did the thing every good person would do, stepped up to go help him. I charged in and kicked and punched them kind of saving our guy and then there comes 2 more. I was basically was fighting 6 people and was happy to see my friends save others. I was getting hit really bad when I heard a person I was fighting say how are you alive. I catched it, he was the boss of them all, maybe that is way I was getting hit hard like hell. I saw many people from our side come to me, one of them said "all are down only them six remains!" I was fighting hard even though I was covered in blood in real this time. They were close and I thought I was saved when. The boss shoot me from his gun. I saw my friends come for me and the good guys take over the bad but... One of them said "We did it!" and I smiled. The guy I saved was the one we found when we were behind the bars for the first time, we met again. I saw everybody and that was the last thing I saw!!! My eyes closed... One month later my eyes opened in a hospital and I see everybody I want to. Looks like I was in a coma and was thinking like I was living it, rare huh. I looked around temporarily disabled but was able to say "We won!!!"

The Author

Read these 2 too if you like.

1) THE LEGEND OF NEKRóS LIEWEG
2) A Havana ooh na-na Journey

Subscribe on YouTube
@Charging world
@Seecaty editz

9 798887 045474

Printed by Libri Plureos GmbH in Hamburg, Germany